For Perrine, Charlotte, and Sophie
Marie H. Henry

First North American Edition

English-language translation by Susan Danon

First published in France in 1990 by Editions Pastel,
an imprint of l'école des loisirs

ISBN 0-316-08654-1

Library of Congress Catalog Card Number 90-53300

Library of Congress Cataloging-in-Publication information is available.

10 9 8 7 6 5 4 3 2 1

Published simultaneously in Canada by
Little, Brown & Company (Canada) Limited

Printed in Belgium

The Rescue of
Brown Bear and White Bear

by Martine Beck
Illustrated by Marie H. Henry

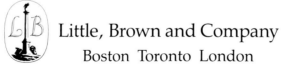
Little, Brown and Company
Boston Toronto London

Ever since their wedding, Brown Bear and White Bear had been living happily in their chalet high in the mountains. One day as they were returning home from the market with some crusty french bread and some fresh vegetables in a basket, warm raindrops began to fall lightly, melting the snow.

"It must be the end of winter," said White Bear.

"Doesn't the forest smell good when it rains!" added Brown Bear.
They quickly removed their soaked boots and their wet clothes so as
not to catch cold . . .

. . . and lit a log fire in the fireplace.
Once he had warmed up a bit, Brown Bear put on his chef's apron
and prepared an enormous pot of spaghetti with tomato-and-basil sauce.

That evening, they played a game of chess on the board that Brown Bear had made out of pieces of gray slate and white marble. As soon as Brown Bear saw that he was losing, he yawned and declared that he was falling asleep.

Cozily snuggled up in their soft feather bed, Brown Bear and White Bear read to each other before going to sleep.

They were suddenly awakened in the middle of the night by a loud rumbling noise. Everything around them began to shake . . .

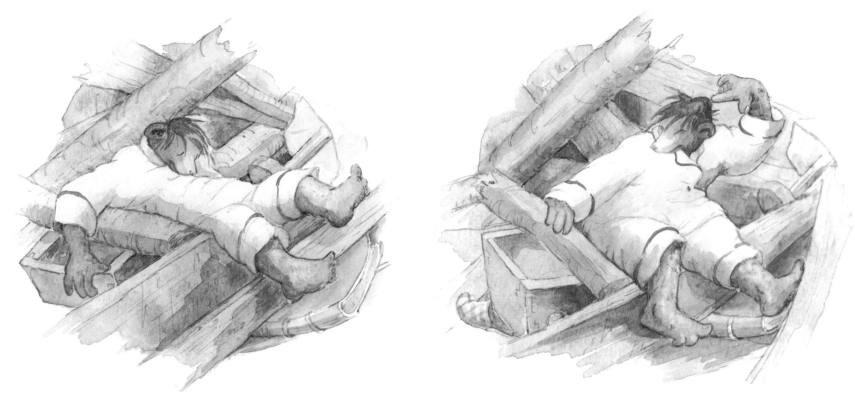

Then it was silent. Brown Bear recovered quite quickly. He pulled himself free from under the beams that were pinning him down and rushed over to his wife. White Bear lay motionless.

An owl perched in a larch tree near the chalet had seen the terrible river of snow sweep away nearly everything in its path. It had almost carried off Brown Bear and White Bear's house. The owl flew off to the village to spread the news.

"Help!" she screeched. "Brown Bear and White Bear's house has been crushed by the avalanche." The villagers grabbed picks, pitchforks, and shovels, then hurried to the ruined chalet.

There was nothing left of the house but a tangle of beams and logs.
The windowpanes were all shattered. The villagers freed White Bear
from the rubble. Luckily, she had only fainted.

To revive her, the rescuers made her drink a small cup of sparkling mountain tonic, while some other bears bandaged up Brown Bear, who would have greatly preferred to have been given a more bracing tonic!

Then the villagers brought some blankets and a pot of tasty pumpkin soup to warm up everyone.

As evening fell, they set up a tent to protect Brown Bear and White Bear from the cold.

"How will I ever be able to thank you for all you have done?" called out Brown Bear as he watched them set off for the village.

The very next day, the villagers piled up planks, nails, axes, and saws in a cart—all that would be necessary to rebuild the chalet—and made their way up the steep path.

Brown Bear and White Bear were just finishing breakfast when they caught sight of the bears coming up the mountain. Soon everyone set to work.

Crash, crash, crash . . . Bang, bang, bang . . .
The sound of sawing, nailing, sandpapering, scraping, hammering,
whistling, puffing and blowing, chatting, and singing was heard . . .

. . . as little by little, the chalet took shape.

White Bear began to feel tired. She was dizzy and felt a bit sick.
"Why am I so sleepy?" she wondered.

Brown Bear was worried and asked her, "What's the matter?"

"I'm not sure, but I think maybe . . ."

"Do you really think so? Are we going to have a baby bear? Our own little bear!" said Brown Bear, very excited.

White Bear rested for hours dreaming of the baby bear she could feel moving about inside her.

Sometimes, when she woke up a bit, she would check on the progress of the house.

At last, the chalet was completed. A little pine tree was placed on the roof and everyone joined in a housewarming party to celebrate.

"Our house is even more beautiful than before!" sighed White Bear contentedly, leaning her head on Brown Bear's shoulder.

Now the two could prepare for the new baby. Brown Bear built a pretty rocking cradle and White Bear embroidered a green pine tree on its pillow.

That evening, after a delicious, candle-lit dinner, they watched a fascinating program about polar bears.

A few weeks later, White Bear was singing some opera, accompanied by Brown Bear on the piano, when she knew the baby bear was getting ready to be born!

Brown Bear called the local midwife: "Come quickly, our baby is about to be born!" White Bear, however, insisted on finishing her knitting. She was making a present — a little jacket for the baby bear!

A few hours later, Brown Bear and White Bear's son was born. They named him Balibar. "You are the most beautiful baby bear in the world," said Brown Bear to his son. And White Bear agreed.